**Dedicated to angels everywhere
who comfort young hearts.**

PAINTING SUNSETS
WITH THE
ANGELS

Vann Wesson
Charla Bergman

*A special thank-you to Lu Kupersmith for her initial creative designs,
and to those wonderful teachers at Francis Parker School
who generously guided us.*

Text copyright © 1996 by Vann Wesson
Illustrations copyright © 1996 by Moira Michaels

All rights reserved.

No part of this publication may be reproduced or transmitted in any form or by any means electronic or mechanical, including photocopy, recording, or any information storage and retrieval system, without permission in writing from the publisher.

Requests for permission to make copies of any part of the work should be mailed to:

Orion Media
3990 Old Town Avenue, Suite 304C
San Diego, California 92110

If you would like to share your comments with us or obtain additional copies. please call us at 1-800-813-3533.

ISBN: 1-887754-04-0

First edition

6 7 8 9 0 1 2 3 4 5 • 9 8 7 6 5 4 3 2 1

Assistant Editor: Anna Roach

Production by Seaside Publishing Services/Printed in Singapore

Publisher Cataloging-in-Publication Data

Wesson, Vann
  Painting sunsets with the angels/written by Vann Wesson; illustrated by Moira Michaels.—1st ed.
   p. cm.
  LCCN: 96-90014
  ISBN: 1-887754-04-0

  SUMMARY: With the help of an angel, David finds a way to bring comfort and peace to his sister, Julia, so she can be happy again after his death.

  1. Children and death—Juvenile fiction. 2. Bereavement in children—Juvenile fiction.
  3. Angels—Juvenile fiction. 4. Religious fiction. I. Michaels, Moira, ill. II. Title.

PS3573.E886P35 1996   [Fic]
                        QBI96-20197

Painting Sunsets
with the
Angels

WRITTEN BY
Vann Wesson

ILLUSTRATED BY
Moira Michaels

ORION MEDIA

Where is Heaven and where do the stars come from?
David knew.
He figured it out one day while sitting in his wheelchair out on the hospital terrace.

David had a disease that would one day take his life.

He was so ill, that he couldn't walk or run like other children. He always had to sit in his wheelchair or lie in his bed. If you had to spend your life the same way, you would probably do a lot of thinking, and ask a lot of questions.

Well, that's what David did.

There were two questions he asked of everyone at least once.

"Where is Heaven, and what are the Stars?"

The answers he was given were usually, "I'm not sure where Heaven is, and the Stars are really Suns just like our own Sun."

David had his own answers.

He thought that the earth was surrounded by a big shell, just like an egg shell surrounds an egg yolk. The outside of the shell was the floor for Heaven where all of the angels live. It sure seemed that way.

That would explain the stars. They were just little holes in the floor of Heaven that light shined through when the Earth was dark and some of the Angels were up late, talking or cleaning their paint brushes and polishing their harps.

Sure, and the beautiful sunsets he sometimes saw through the big windows at the foot of his bed were paintings that the Angels made on the sky shell just before they turned out the great big light that everyone called the Sun.

Of all the sunsets, he loved the fiery red and purple ones that came in the summer best. He thought that maybe the Angels had more time to spend painting them because the Sun stayed around longer in the summertime.

David knew that someday soon he might die. But he really didn't feel like crying about it anymore, because now he had a special secret. He knew he would go to Heaven and become a well and healthy Angel. Then he would be able to jump and play with the other Angel children, and would never have to sit in a wheelchair again.

Every day David's mother, father, and sister Julia came to the hospital to see him.

Each morning they brought his breakfast and visited with him during the day.

Each evening they tucked him into bed after he said his prayers.

Julia sometimes became very sad when she remembered that David might die soon.
But then one day . . .

David told her his secret.

One night an Angel had come to see David and had spoken to him.

David said, "I asked the Angel to please let me be one of the Angels who paints the sunsets. I told the Angel that I wouldn't mind cleaning up the paint brushes and canvases. I would be very neat and I wouldn't make any messes either."

The Angel told David that all of the Angels had been watching over him and already knew what he wanted to do when he got to Heaven.

They all thought David would be a great sunset painter and the Angel told him not to worry about it. He could do whatever he wanted to do.

One morning when David's family came to bring him breakfast, they found that David had gone to be with the Angels.

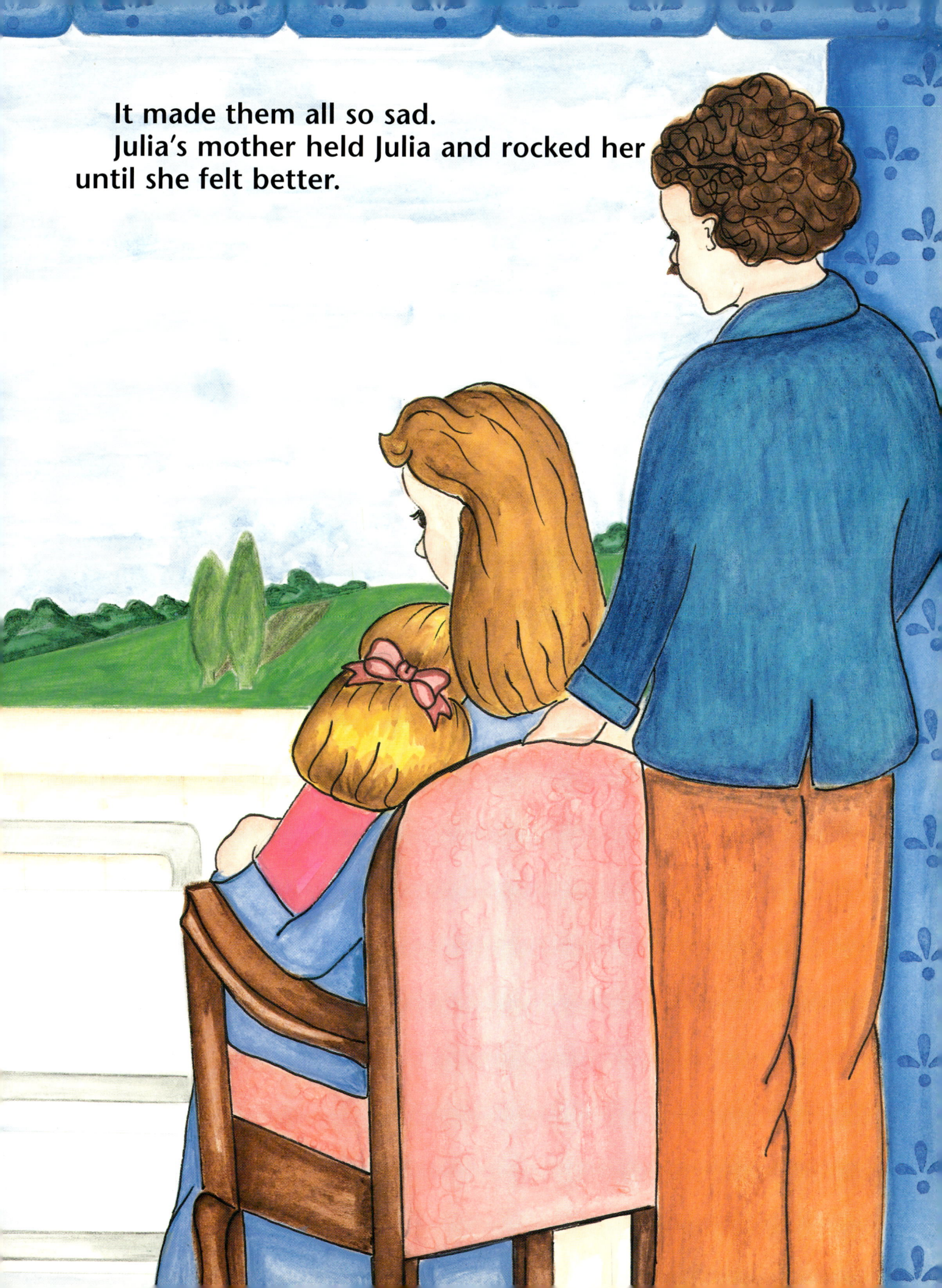

It made them all so sad.
Julia's mother held Julia and rocked her until she felt better.

A few days later they had a funeral for David.

His mother, father, Julia, the doctors and nurses, and all of the other people who knew him were there.
They were all very sad.
They would all miss David.

Julia and her mother and father stayed at the cemetery long after everyone else had gone home.

Finally Julia said, "Good-bye David, I'll miss you, but I know you're happy now."

That evening, when Julia was outside watching a beautiful summer sunset with her mother and father, she thought of David, and it made her feel a little sad all over again.

But then she saw something in the sky that made her smile, and chased away her sadness.

Julia knew David was telling her that everything was okay. She didn't need to be sad about him anymore. He was having fun painting sunsets with the Angels.

From then on, whenever Julia saw a sunset, she thought of her happy brother, David.